O-SONO and the magician's nephew and the elephant

by Henry Morgan

illustrated by Spanfeller

An Edward Ernest Book

The Vanguard Press, Inc.

for my mother

Shortly before once upon a time, in a country quite far from 'most anyplace, there lived a truly unusual princess. She was unusual because a princess is just *supposed* to be terribly beautiful — but this one really was. Her name was O-Sono. She was also called "The Pearl in the Lotus" and "Daughter of the Seven Perfumes." Her father, a wealthy emperor, called her "Daughter."

This emperor, Bom Bay Dukk, had a shiny mahogany palace that was polished once a month with essence of lemon verbena, and it smelled fine. There was a big porch all around the palace and inside were dozens of rooms, some of which were simply gorgeous. The rest were magnificent. One room was lined with silk, another with pretty feathers, and one had a tiny ocean in it with a fine sandy beach and a hot-dog stand. A hot dog cost five rollolios, but the rollolio isn't worth anything in our money so everything was free.

For breakfast, the Emperor ate what you eat for lunch. For lunch, he ate what you eat for dinner. And for dinner, he had eleven ice-cream sodas, saving the best one for dessert.

Sometimes it's hard work being an emperor, especially in the summer, and once in a while, after a particularly bad day, the Emperor would come out on the porch in the green and blue evening, kick off his shoes, and he and his daughter would sit in rocking chairs and eat watermelon.

Now, the Emperor had some wonderful possessions. He had two roast-beef trees, both very rare, and a fine set of china, made in Japan. He had fireflies of many colors — puce, magenta, olive drab, and persimmon — and a horse that could count to seventeen. He had three refrigerators. Two were kept filled with lemonade, while the third had more sugar, in case someone needed it.

And the Emperor had a jungle. It was the finest jungle you ever saw — two miles long and two blocks wide, with a little fence around it so you could tell where it started. The jungle was full of fascinating things: red-and-green zebras, checkered zebras, zebras of all one color. And there were bell birds that went *ding-dong*, gypsy birds that played the fiddle, flute birds that went *toodle-oodle*, a drum bird that said *boom*, and a piano bird for accompaniment.

And there was a herd of elephants. One of the girl elephants, Selma, was sixteen years old and very pretty. She had violet eyes, long, dark lashes, and a peaches-and-cream complexion. She walked with delicate steps. And sometimes she blushed. At night she slept under a weeping willow. During the day she sighed. She was lonesome. You see, she was so lovely that the boy elephants thought she was too good for them, so they never said hello. The girl elephants wouldn't speak to her because they were jealous, and they said she was "stuck-up." She *wasn't*. She was just shy and unhappy and lonesome and didn't know what to do about it.

Now, in the palace there also lived a magician. He was a jolly little man with a head like a honeydew melon. He had a room of his own where he kept all the things a magician has to have if he wants to get anywhere in life: a stuffed kangaroo; some dusty old bottles filled with peach juice and sesame seeds; rabbits that spent the day appearing and disappearing; a thing that looked like a cow's tail but wasn't; a machine for making it snow; a hat shaped like an ice-cream cone upside down, with stars and a moon on it; an owl that said "Who, me?"; a strawberry-colored cat; and a bureau full of odds and ends. The magician's name was Ho Lee Kow, and he practiced magic for two hours every Monday afternoon. His newest trick was to mix yellow stuff and blue stuff, hoping to make green stuff. But no matter what he mixed with what, all he ever got was hot coffee.

Ho Lee Kow had a nephew named Chan, who worked as his apprentice. And Chan was in love. It seems that one day, while walking in the garden at twilight, he heard a voice singing, and it sounded like a hundred silver bells floating in perfume. Following the sound, he came to a beautiful ivory gate, and beyond the gate there was a path that led to an enchanted pool. All about were flamingo trees with leaves of pink feathers, and clusters of pussy-cat plants. In the pool swam a lavender swan, and off to one side, in a little clearing among the cowslips and bluebells, was a bench made of gold and crystal. And on this glittering bench sat O-Sono, daughter of the Emperor.

Chan took a step. O-Sono turned and smiled at him. There was a moment of almost-silence. Away in the distance they could hear the Emperor's nightingale giving his heart to the rising moon.

Finally Chan spoke. He whispered, "You are the Princess O-Sono."

The Princess blushed and pretended to be looking at her slippers. Then she said "Yes," in a voice so soft that it might have been the wind in the grass.

"I am Chan, the magician's apprentice."

"I know," the Princess said — or maybe it was a breeze in the ferns.

Again there was a moment of almost-silence. The lavender swan drifted by, and a tiny wave broke on the shore of the enchanted pool. At last Chan, looking deep into the eyes of O-Sono, took her hand and said, "I have this moment fallen in love forever."

Chan sat down beside the Princess and they held pinkies. They blushed a little and then they laughed and then they blushed and then they laughed.

A baby bee buzzed by. The setting sun smiled at some daisies and the daisies smiled back. A tiny tree frog sang four bars of "*Vesti la Giubba*" and then fell asleep.

And sitting there on the gold-and-crystal bench beside the enchanted pool in the most magical twilight ever made, the Princess and the magician's apprentice decided to be married.

The very next day, O-Sono went to the throne room to tell her father of her love for Chan. When she had spoken, the Emperor's face darkened with anger. "What?" he cried. "My daughter, the daughter of the Emperor Bom Bay Dukk, marry a magician — and only an apprentice magician, at that?" The Emperor turned purple. "Never!" he shouted. "I shall never permit it. Not in forty-two billion, trillion, squad-rillion years!"

Turning to the court physician, he roared, "Bring me two aspirins!" And the court physician hurried away.

Then the Emperor pointed at his daughter. "As for you," he said, "you are going to have no dessert for one week. You are not to go near the enchanted pool. And from now on you will spend two hours a day learning to play the oboe."

Two of the most beautiful tears in the world filled the Princess's eyes. She turned and left the throne room. She was in deepest, deepest despair.

Chan did not hear the sad news right away because he had gone for a walk in the jungle. It was a lovely day, all curly and shining. The sun was pouring more butter into the buttercups. A dragonfly flew up and down between two rows of hollyhocks, stitching them together. Off to one side a little brook ran chuckling over the stones.

As Chan rounded a sharp turn in the path, he suddenly came upon Selma, the beautiful girl elephant. She was sitting under an angel-cake tree, and there were tears in her eyes.

"For goodness' sake!" said Chan, and he just stared at her. "Aren't you going to say hello?" he asked. "Why are you crying? What are you doing here all alone?"

Selma looked at him and decided he was very nice. Slowly she said, "I'm alone — that is, I'm always alone because I . . . well, because I . . . I really don't know anybody else . . ." and her voice trailed away.

"Don't know anybody else?" said Chan. "Why, that's astonishing! That's amazing! But if you'd like to *start* knowing somebody, you can start with me. Let's be friends, and then you can always come and talk to me."

Selma looked even unhappier than before. "I'd like to be your friend," she said in a small voice, "but I've never been one. I don't know how to act. I don't know what to say or what to do. I . . . I just don't know what a friend *does*."

"Oh," said Chan, "it's easy . . . .

A friend knows your troubles and says 'There, there!'
And holds your hand and pats your hair
And lends you a hanky for your eyes.
A friend gives you grape juice and peppermint pies . . .
He takes your side in case there's a fight,
And when you're wrong he says you're right!

"I would do all those things for you and even lots more," said Chan, "and all you have to do is just be you, and when we see each other we'll be glad, and then we'll be friends. All right?"

Selma was delighted. She was so happy to have a friend that she almost whistled — but naturally elephants *can't* whistle. So Selma patted Chan's head with her trunk, and they agreed to meet again the following Thursday. Boys *can* whistle, of course, and Chan waved good-by and walked away whistling merrily.

Suddenly a dark cloud wiped out the sun. Suddenly there was a chill in the air. And just as suddenly, a messenger from the palace appeared on the path ahead.

"Chan, I have bad news," the messenger said, and he hung his head. "I'm sorry to tell you this, but the Emperor will not consent to your marriage with the Princess. He says that no daughter of his will ever marry a third-rate magician." Then the messenger, embarrassed, turned and ran back in the direction of the palace.

Chan stood very still. He was shocked. And hurt. And depressed. And mortified, upset, angry, sad, sulky, fretful, wounded, and sullen. And he wasn't happy about being called a third-rate magician, either. *Wait a minute! Third-rate magician!* He frowned and looked at the ground and thought about it. Maybe the Emperor was right! Then the answer was simple: Become a *first*-rate magician! Didn't his uncle have all the equipment to learn with? Of course! The thing to do was to rush back to the palace and begin learning immediately.

The dark cloud slid past the sun and the day grew lovely again. A bullfrog croaked "Hurrah!" and a flag bird waved by. Chan hurried to the palace, across the porch, through the door, and up the stairs to his uncle's room. As he opened the door, he saw at once that something important was going on. There was a big pot bubbling over a fire, and all the magician's helpers were bustling about. Ho Lee Kow was poking into jars and boxes, and it was perfectly clear that something terribly magic was about to happen. The owl flew from the bureau to the top of the window shade and said "Who, me?" four times. A magician second-class was stirring something in a china cup. Two elves were jumping up and down trying to see into the pot. On the table was a big yellow book with a title in bold black letters: FIVE EASY TRICKS AND FIVE HARD ONES.

Ho Lee Kow was ready to go to work.

Now, it's true that Ho wasn't the best magician in the world. It's also true that he wasn't second best. Maybe eleventh or thirty-eighth. Anyway, he threw more and more things into the bubbling pot: half a can of polly seeds; five cents' worth of blubber; a heaping tablespoonful of a secret ingredient; a bar of solid gold; and at least twenty-two other mysterious, magical things. Finally, all was ready. Everybody gathered around the bubbling pot.

Then Ho raised his magic wand and said "Passamaquoddy Hopatcong" three times. Suddenly there was a loud BOOM! Sparks flew in every direction, a huge cloud rose from the pot, and everyone in the room was covered from head to foot with sawdust. There in the bottom of the pot was . . . hot coffee! Again! Poor Chan turned away sadly. He realized that if he were ever to learn a good solid magic trick, his uncle was not the one to teach him. He would just have to study by himself.

A few minutes later the Emperor heard that the trick had been
a failure. Some sneak had told him. And so the Emperor felt that
he had been quite right in the first place: Why allow his daughter
to marry the nephew of a magician who wasn't really very good to
begin with? Yes, the Emperor was extremely pleased — so pleased,
in fact, that he recited his favorite poem, one he had written in
honor of himself:

TO A PERFECTLY MARVELOUS EMPEROR

Oh, boy! Who is smarter than the King of Cathay?
Who is keener than the Duke of Toolay?
Who, I say, is brighter than they?
I am he. It is me.
No, that's wrong. Let me see . . .
It is I!
Who is cuter than the Earl of Carruther?
Who knows lots more than his own grandmother?
But certainly! Who else could it be?
I am he. It is me.
No, that's wrong. Let me see . . .
It is I!

On Thursday, Chan went to the jungle to meet Selma. The elephant was delighted to see him, and they talked for hours about this and that. Then they talked about things in general. They talked about what was going on here and there and then went back to this and that. They agreed that spring was best but that they certainly had a lot of fun in the summer.

Suddenly Chan had an idea. "I should have thought of this before," he said, "but I didn't. I have a friend who would love to meet you!"

"Meet *me*?" said Selma, blushing prettily. "I don't really think I'm quite re—"

"Nonsense," Chan interrupted her. "My friend will love you just as much as I do." And he explained about the Princess O-Sono, and finally Selma agreed to go to the edge of the jungle to meet her.

As the boy and the lovely elephant walked along, everybody in the jungle seemed to be saying hello. The palm trees waved slowly and gracefully. A jolly breeze kissed their cheeks and then ran on to say "Good day" to some violets. Some giant sunflowers nodded a little. They were either saying hello or taking a nap. A bluebird sat in a clump of blueberries, and they didn't see him at all. Once a periwinkle bird flew by. No one had ever seen one before . . . no one has seen one since.

At last they came to the edge of the jungle. "Wait here," said Chan. "I'll be back in a minute." And he went off to fetch O-Sono.

In thirty-two seconds he returned, and the Princess was with him. O-Sono looked at Selma. Selma looked at O-Sono. And both of them said, at the very same time, "Why, she's beautiful!" And then everybody laughed.

Now, the Princess was very intelligent. And at this moment her face brightened and her eyes sparkled as an idea suddenly struck her. She moved close to Chan. "Listen, dear," she said to him, and then she whispered something in his ear. This was very rude, but once in a while a princess can be rude and nobody notices. You see, everybody knows that a princess is never rude, so when she is, it doesn't count.

Chan's face lit up as he listened to O-Sono. He turned to Selma and said, "Selma, our dear friend, meet us here two days from today at six o'clock. We'll have a surprise for you." And so it was

agreed.

Now, it happened that two days later it was sort-of-April and time for the Emperor's biggest party of the year. He just loved to give a sort-of-April party, and people were invited from all over. The Emperor of Edelweiss came with his mother. The Crown Prince of Titipu came, and so did the mighty Analect of Kwang-fu-tze, the pretender to the throne of Bublitchki, various aunts and uncles, and people met on trips to the country, and people who happened to be around, and people who just liked parties.

It was a perfect day for the party — sunny and bright and filled with the fragrance of flowers. The whole outside of the shiny mahogany palace had been newly polished with essence of lemon verbena, and the inside looked like Christmas in fairyland. The Emperor sat on his peacock throne, and pretty ladies sat on the steps. The Emperor's brother-in-law had a lovely seat in the balcony, where he could see everything very clearly — if he bent his neck just a little.

At last everyone was seated in the throne room, and it was time for the entertainment. First all the guests had to sing the Emperor's old school song. While they sang, the Emperor played his potato whistle. Then everyone sat down and waiters came out and served watercress buns and bottles of root beer. Later there would be more things to eat and drink, but now it was time for the parade of the musicians. The Emperor clapped his hands, and in came a white pony with a black tail, pulling a little cart with a huge harp in the

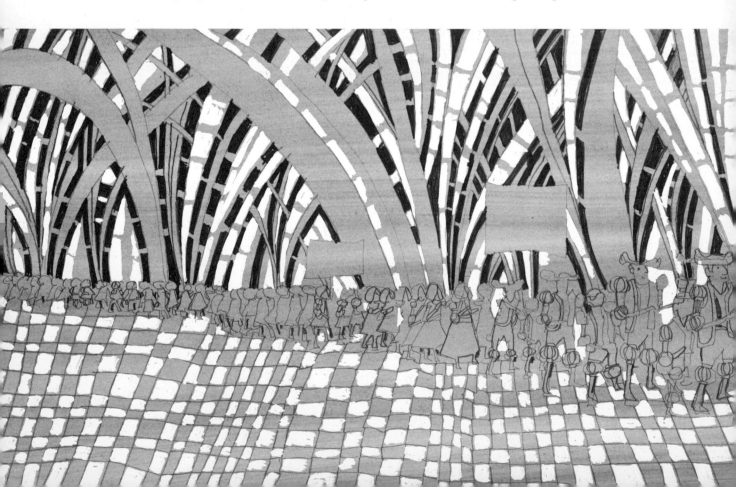

back. A man seven feet tall walked behind, playing the harp. Next came a hundred little boys wearing music racks for hats, with a sheet of music on each rack. In back of them marched a hundred Swiss bell ringers, reading the music and swinging their bells. They were followed by five hundred girls playing combs covered with tissue paper. And then came the sweet-potato band, the kazoo men, the accordion players, and others too numerous to mention. The huge throne room rang with the sound of the music. It was magnificent!

After the parade of the musicians, the waiters came out again and served hot chestnuts, ladyfingers, marmalade on muffins, and apricot juice in tall glasses. When everybody had wiped his hands on hot towels, the Emperor rang a little bell, the big doors opened, and in came Ho Lee Kow and all his helpers. Chan, too. It was time for the magic tricks.

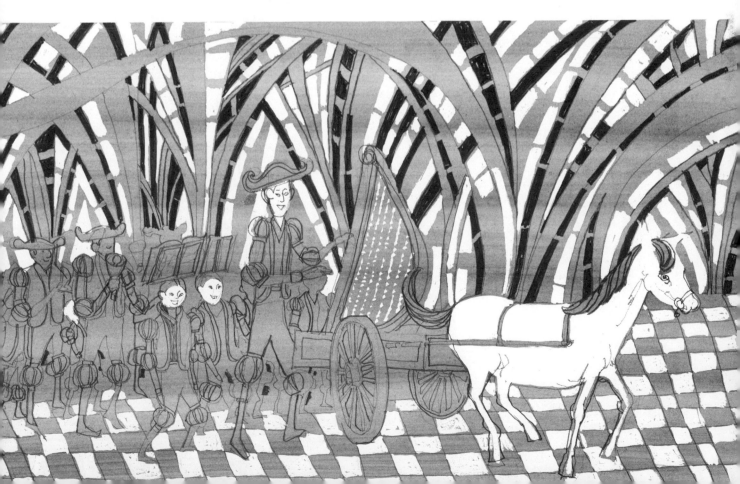

"Emperor," said Ho, "some of my magic hasn't worked out too well lately, so today my nephew, Chan, will do some tricks instead. Anyway," he said, "he deserves a chance, because last week he got ninety-five in spelling."

The Princess O-Sono leaned forward eagerly in her seat near the peacock throne. She looked anxiously at her father. The Emperor frowned and hesitated. First he said "No." Then he said "Yes." And finally Chan went to the center of the floor.

He began by doing a few simple card tricks to make everyone feel comfortable. Then he did the other easy ones, like turning fire into water and pulling a monkey out of a cap. The guests clapped politely. They had seen all these tricks before. Then Chan's helpers brought in the big iron pot and made a fire under it. Chan backed away, made a few mysterious motions with his arms, and then threw a little purple powder into the pot. Suddenly there was an ear-shattering explosion and the whole hall was filled with smoke. As the smoke cleared, everybody in the room went "OHHHH!" For there, next to the big iron pot, stood Selma, blinking and blushing! The Emperor was astonished. "Why," he exclaimed, "that is the greatest trick I've ever seen in my life! My boy, you are amazing! This is . . . why, this is a miracle!"

Selma blushed more than ever and said "Good gracious!" Everybody laughed and applauded, and Selma felt a lot better.

Chan was even more astonished by his trick than the Emperor was, and while all the guests were laughing and applauding, he slipped up to Selma and whispered, "Selma! How did you get in here? You were supposed to meet O-Sono and me at six o'clock at the edge of the jungle."

Selma waved her trunk shyly and whispered back, "I guess having two friends has made me very brave. I was walking by the edge of the jungle and I heard all the music and the clapping and I wanted to see what was happening at the palace. So I wandered over and no one was at the door and I just followed my trunk to the throne room." She paused and looked down at her feet. "I don't know what's going on, but I'm very pleased that everyone likes me."

"Everyone *loves* you!" said Chan, and he gave the beautiful girl elephant a big hug. "And we're going to prove it!" Chan whispered in O-Sono's ear, and she turned and whispered excitedly to one of her ladies-in-waiting, who nodded and ran quickly out of the throne room.

The Emperor was so pleased with Chan's trick that he announced then and there that he thought the boy would make a wonderful son-in-law. And to be sure that Chan would never have to worry about his allowance again, the Emperor gave him nearly half his kingdom. He gave him the river that flows to the sea, and the mountains called "The White-Haired Grandfathers." He gave him beautiful farms and fruitful orchards, and he gave him two gold mines and a castle and a baby duck and a box of skyrockets. And, most important of all, he gave him O-Sono.

Chan was overwhelmed. He turned to O-Sono and took her hand. She smiled the smile of a thousand lights. The guests in the throne room cheered and clapped and stamped their feet. Then suddenly Chan held up his hand for silence, and in the hush that followed he said, "My noble Emperor, ladies and gentlemen of the court. My lovely bride-to-be. Everybody. You couldn't see how that trick was done because of all the smoke in the room, but it really was very simple to do and I'm not very proud of it. But if you will all bear with me for a moment, I would like to try to do what I think is really the most difficult trick in the world. It has never been done before."

Now, what Chan had said was absolutely true. He was about to try something that needed even more than magic. It needed Faith and it needed Hope and it needed a beautiful heart. And it needed every bit of concentration a boy could possibly have.

Chan whispered to his helpers and they rushed to get the fire going under the pot again. When everything was ready, Chan raised his arms and concentrated very hard. He mumbled to himself, concentrated very hard again, and threw some more purple powder into the iron pot. Immediately there was a huge BOOM! Once again the hall was filled with smoke . . . and everybody stood breathless. As the smoke began to clear, they saw . . . they saw . . . and now, perfectly clear . . . *another elephant!* Handsome! Proud! Strong! The most beautiful *boy* elephant in the whole world!

This was beyond doubt the most marvelous trick that had ever been done by anybody. It was exactly what Chan had tried to do but he would never, never know just what had happened. He was astonished and pleased, thoughtful and tearful, and grateful and laughing and completely joyous. "How perfect!" he said. "What is your name?"

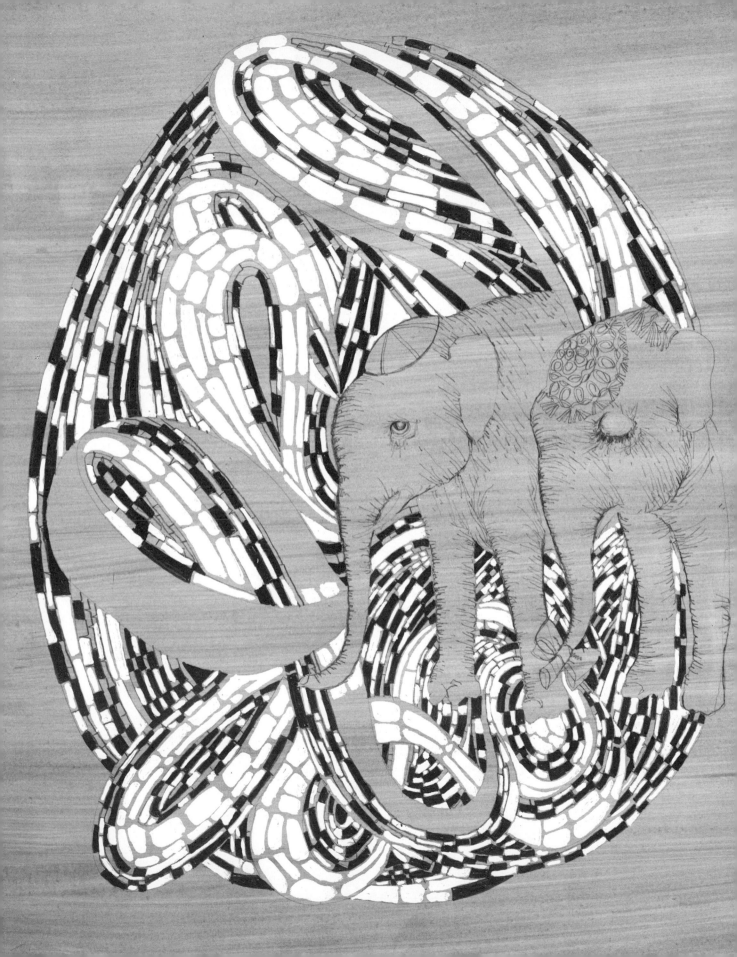

"Harold," said the boy elephant.

Harold looked at Selma. She blushed. She looked at the ground. She was happy!

Chan and the Princess O-Sono held hands tightly. O-Sono smiled the smile of a thousand springtimes, bowed to her father and the court, and said, "Oh, most noble Emperor, my father, you see now how wonderful is magic. Of course, we just *call* it magic, and we all know that it is really dreams and hopes and happy thoughts and warm loving-kindness. Magic is the mystery and wonder of life that can come only from the human heart."

After this lovely speech all the people in the throne room applauded very loudly and then got up and smoothed their clothes. One by one they went and said "Thank you" and "Good-by" to the Emperor and O-Sono and Chan, and then they went home. It was the best sort-of-April party the Emperor had ever had.

And Chan and O-Sono still live in the country quite far from 'most anyplace. They walk often in the garden and sit on the gold-and-crystal bench by the enchanted pool. They watch the lavender swan float by and they listen to the tiny tree frog sing. And nearly every week they stop by the angel-cake tree in the jungle and visit the most beautiful girl elephant and the most handsome boy elephant in the world. They are very, very happy.